in a deep, deep valley in a dark, dark cave...

могущественный

there lived a mighty dragon.

He could fly higher than the clouds

and faster than all the birds.

He could burn down a forest

with a blast of his fiery breath.

He could smash a castle wall

with a flick of his mighty tail.

And he could brush away an army

with a sweep of his monstrous wing.

There was nothing so fierce and so terrible
as the mighty dragon.

But he had a secret. A big secret, well, actually, a very small secret...

he was terrified of mice!

Which was a pity, because that very day a mouse moved into the cave just next door.

His name was George.

Now, George didn't much care for the cave next door. It was cold and dark and draughty.

The previous owner had been a bat,
so the fixtures and furnishings were
most inconvenient.

And the nearest cheese shop was
miles and miles away.

George was feeling rather miserable.
And to make matters worse...

he had NO SUGAR for his tea!

'I know,' said George, 'I'll just pop next
door and see if I can borrow some.'
So he did.

'I say, you couldn't loan me a couple of lumps of sugar, could you?' asked George.

'AAAAAAAAAGH!' screamed the dragon.

And fled.

'Oh, blow,' groaned George. 'No tea, then.'

But George did get his tea after all, with
two lumps of sugar. And he got cheese, too.
And nuts and berries and biscuits and

crackers and cream cheese sandwiches and jelly and ice cream and fairy cakes with pink icing and...

a cosy little hole in the castle wall.

To John and Terry

PUFFIN BOOKS

UK | USA | Canada | Ireland | Australia
India | New Zealand | South Africa

Puffin Books is part of the Penguin Random House group of companies
whose addresses can be found at global.penguinrandomhouse.com.

www.penguin.co.uk
www.puffin.co.uk
www.ladybird.co.uk

Penguin
Random House
UK

First published by Jonathan Cape 2002
Published by Red Fox 2003
This edition published 2019

001

Printed in China

A CIP catalogue record for this book is available from the British Library

ISBN: 978–0–241–37040–7

All correspondence to:
Puffin Books, Penguin Random House Children's
80 Strand, London WC2R 0RL